The Invisible Leash

Patrice Karst Illustrated by Joanne Lew-Vriethoff

L B
Little, Brown and Company
New York   Boston

The illustrations for this book were created digitally. This book was designed by Véronique Lefèvre Sweet.
The production was supervised by Erika Schwartz, and the production editor was Annie McDonnell.
The text was set in Shannon, and the display type is Gulyesa.

Little, Brown and Company, Hachette Book Group, 1290 Avenue of the Americas, New York, NY 10104
Visit us at LBYR.com

Originally published in hardcover and ebook by Little, Brown and Company in December 2019
First Trade Paperback Edition: May 2021

Little, Brown and Company is a division of Hachette Book Group, Inc.
The Little, Brown name and logo are trademarks of Hachette Book Group, Inc.

The publisher is not responsible for websites (or their content) that are not owned by the publisher.

The Library of Congress has cataloged the hardcover edition as follows:
Names: Karst, Patrice, author. | Lew-Vriethoff, Joanne, illustrator.
Title: The Invisible Leash / by Patrice Karst ; illustrated by Joanne Lew-Vriethoff.
Description: First edition. | New York ; Boston : Little, Brown and Company, 2019. | Summary: Emily tries to comfort her best friend,
Zack, whose dog Jojo recently died, by telling him about the "Invisible Leash" that connects each owner to his or her deceased pet.
Identifiers: LCCN 2018023817| ISBN 9780316524858 (hardcover) | ISBN 9780316524902 (ebook) | ISBN 9780316524865 (library edition ebook)
Subjects: | CYAC: Loss (Psychology)—Fiction. | Death—Fiction. | Pets—Fiction. | Best friends—Fiction. | Friendship—Fiction.
Classification: LCC PZ7.K1513 Ik 2019 | DDC [E]—dc23
LC record available at https://lccn.loc.gov/2018023817

ISBNs: 978-0-316-52489-6 (pbk.), 978-0-316-52487-2 (ebook), 978-0-316-52490-2 (ebook), 978-0-316-52484-1 (ebook)

Printed in China

APS

10 9 8 7 6 5

"Ready to go, Zack?" Emily asked her friend. It was Friday and the rest of the kids were already racing home from school, excited for the weekend. Zack shook his head. He just wanted to be alone.

"Okay, but let's hang out at the tree house later," Emily said, leaving him at his desk. The only thoughts in Zack's mind were of Jojo, as he slung his heavy backpack over his shoulder and slowly headed home.

This weekend, Jojo wouldn't be there.

Jojo had been Zack's best friend in the whole world. They played Frisbee on the weekends.

Together they hiked the hills and trails near Zack's house.

And when the moon was full, they howled together as it smiled down upon them.

Mom and Dad tried to cheer Zack up with his favorite rainbow cupcakes. But Jojo wasn't there to steal the very last bite.

"Cupcakes aren't the same without Jojo," Zack said, and pushed his plate away.

"We'll adopt another dog as soon as you're ready, buddy," Dad reassured him.

But Zack wasn't interested. "No other dog, Dad! Never!
I just want Jojo back!"

Zack stomped off and when his bedroom door slammed, it shook the whole house with *sad*.

Before dinner, Emily came by to see if Zack could play.

"Hey, what's wrong, Zack? Why didn't you meet me at the tree house? Come over!"

Emily tugged playfully at Zack's arm, and they began to wind their way through the neighborhood. But Zack dragged his feet.

"Jojo died this week. He got old and sick. Now I'll never see him again. Not ever."

He started to cry.

Emily understood. "It's okay, Zack. I cried so hard when Rexie died too. But then I heard the news."

Zack was curious. "What news?"

Emily had a sparkle in her eyes. "Oh, just **the very best news ever!**"

"Rexie and I will always be connected," Emily continued, "just like you and Jojo!"

"Huh?" Zack blinked. "That makes no sense. How can you be connected to someone that's gone?"

Emily held out her hands.

"Because they're not *all-the-way* gone. See?"

Zack squinted and stared, but he only saw the air. "Are you playing a trick on me? Because I can't see a thing."

"I know, but the Invisible Leash is the realest thing in the whole wide world, Zack. When our pets aren't here anymore,

an Invisible Leash connects our hearts to each other.

Forever."

Zack folded his arms across his chest. "I only believe in things I can see."

A sudden gust of warm breeze blew right through Emily's hair, and she laughed. "But Zack, don't you believe in the wind? Even if you can't see the Invisible Leash, you can feel it. That's what we found out the night that Rexie died."

Zack was getting annoyed. "There is no such thing as an Invisible Leash!"

"Grandpa said his grandpa told him about the Leash when he was a little boy and his dog Louie died. He said it stretches to this place beyond where our eyes can see…

all the way to where our pets have gone."

"Yeah, right. That's totally impossible!" Zack laughed, even though nothing felt funny. None of this seemed like it could be real. But oh, how he wished it could be. "How could Rexie have an Invisible Leash? She's a cat. You never walked her on a leash."

"Not when she was alive, but she has an Invisible Leash now. Just like my sister's bird, Cuckoo, and my brother's hamster, Fred."

"Well, Jojo didn't really like his leash. He loved running free." Zack figured he'd stumped Emily this time. But she still had an answer.

"It's not a Leash that ties our bodies.
It's a Leash that connects our hearts.

When you love an animal and they love you back, that gives the Invisible Leash the magic power of infinity to stretch from here all the way to the beyond."

Zack wanted to know more. "Where exactly is the beyond? Do you mean like another planet way out in space?"

"There and everywhere!" answered Emily. "Grandpa says the beyond can even be all around us. He said that we'd spend the rest of our lives learning that we feel the most important and truest things in the world in our hearts, and don't need to see them with our eyes. That's what it means to believe."

"I wish I could believe, Emily. I wish that so much."

Zack began to wonder as they watched the moon rising over the valley. He remembered how much he and Jojo loved the full moon. "When Jojo misses me, would I feel him tug the Invisible Leash, just like when I used to walk him?"

"Yup," said Emily. "And it works both ways. When I miss Rexie, I tug on the Invisible Leash and sometimes I can even hear her purr!"

"For real?" asked Zack, looking his friend in the eye.

"For very real!" answered Emily. And when she added,
"Cross my heart," Zack knew how much she meant it.

Warm winds swirled around the two friends gazing at the evening sky. Frogs croaked and crickets started chirping as the stars began to gather. Soon, a smile widened across Zack's face.

"Emily, what if Jojo and Rexie have been looking at the very same moon we're looking at...

so they're with us right now?"

"Oh, Zack!" She jumped up. "I never thought of that before. The very same moon! Now I feel Rexie tugging her Invisible Leash this exact second!"

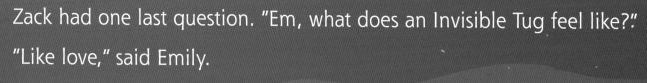

Zack had one last question. "Em, what does an Invisible Tug feel like?"

"Like love," said Emily.

Zack's heart started to feel all kinds of warm. "Well, I think maybe I can feel Jojo tugging me from the beyond."

"Right now?" asked Emily.

"Very right now," answered Zack.

They sat there for a long time with no words.

Then, when it was time for dinner, they hugged goodbye
and the moon lit up Zack's pathway home.

Later that night, Zack looked again at the moon, now glowing full and bright in his window. He was almost positive that he could hear the sound of Jojo beginning to howl, just like he used to. And so...he joined in. When they were done, Zack saw Jojo's sparkling brown eyes looking deeply into his. This did not feel like any dream. This felt real.

And for the first time since Jojo died,

Zack fell asleep happy.

Somewhere even higher than the moon, in a place called *the beyond*, Jojo and Rexie watched their people, Zack and Emily, as they slept.

Jojo ran in circles and barked with joy. "We love our people so much!"

Rexie rolled on the grass, purring. "When our people are happy, we feel happy too!"

The other animals were celebrating alongside them.

One day, the children of the world would know the truth about their Invisible Leashes, which let their animals run free but **connect their hearts forever**.

One day, those children would teach others how to believe in the things that they could feel—yet not quite see.

It was the still of night. Zack, Emily, and the rest of the world's children were now fast asleep in their cozy-comfy beds. And as the moon smiled down upon them from high above, it lit up the millions and billions of Invisible Leashes...

connecting them ALL.

A WORD FROM THE AUTHOR

This book is dedicated to you, my precious little Coco, beloved wiener dog of my heart, you who were always ready to "lick and love up" a new friend. Thank you for the gift of being your momma from the day you leapt into my life at eight weeks old. Throughout all of our adventures—the good, the bad, and the sometimes really bad—you helped me in ways that have no words. You taught me to love like no other four-legged creature on Earth ever could! I feel honored to live my life striving to have as wide open a heart as you did. We always knew that the Invisible Leash is real, but now we get to share our news with the whole wide world!

Dear Reader,

As I worked on the final draft of this book, my little Coco made her very own journey to the beyond. Little did I know how much I would need the comfort of these very pages and the peace they brought to my soul as I grieved her loss. If you are grieving the loss of your beloved companion, this book is especially for you. How very grateful I am to share our story with you now...

Thank you to:

All the fans of *The Invisible String* who asked me for a book that would explain our forever connection to our animals. This book is yours....

My agent dream team, Michelle Zeitlin and Jane Cowen Hamilton of More Zap Literary, for believing in my vision and then bringing it home! Fruition is a beautiful thing....

Andrea Spooner and everyone else at Little, Brown Books for Young Readers for journeying with me into the realms of The Invisible, that we might share them with the world, thereby helping to make them Visible....

Joanne Lew-Vriethoff, my illustrator, for taking my stories and breathing life, heart, and soul into them....

Elijah, my other child (the two-legged one!), who inspired *The Invisible String*. You, Coco, and I will forever remain connected by our Invisible Leash. But then, you already *knew* that....

All creatures great and small and especially the precious pets with whom we intimately share our homes, lives, and hearts, thank you for loving us unconditionally....

And lastly, for creating them in the first place, that we could open our hearts wide with exquisite love for and from the *animals*—a big shout-out to GOD....

Bless the Beasts and the Children,

Love, Patrice